AF430424

MR. CRAB
Sumaya Alhammadi
AUSTIN MACAULEY PUBLISHERS™
LONDON • CAMBRIDGE • NEW YORK • SHARJAH

Copyright © Sumaya Alhammadi (2021)

ISBN – 9789948834526 – (Paperback)
ISBN – 9789948834519 – (E-Book)

Application Number: MC-10-01-3303240
Age Classification: 10-12

The age group that matches the content of the books has been classified according to the age classification system issued by the National Media Council.

First Published (2021)
AUSTIN MACAULEY PUBLISHERS FZE
Sharjah Publishing City
P.O Box: [519201]
Sharjah, UAE
www.austinmacauley.ae
+971 655 95 202

Deep in the ocean, there lived a crab who had a passion for cooking. He wished to own a well-known restaurant and to be a famous chef. This crab was known as Mr. Crab.

So, he started as a novice cooker in
an old and cheap restaurant. From this
job, he earned some money, but he lost
his job as a result of closing
the restaurant.

Mr. Crab felt depressed. He thought that his cooking journey has ended here!

CLOSED

He began his lazy life. The days were spent sleeping, eating, and watching TV programs. He also used to watch TV programs at night and sleep all day.

After serval weeks, Mr. Crab had
nothing to eat and no money to pay his
rent, so he was kicked out from
his house too!

Mr. Crab felt broken. He started walking in the streets thinking about his future, his mind was full of questions like, How will I live without a job?, How will I bury my passion?

SHOP

He spent a night in the street, his smell turned similar to musty, so he started thinking about troubles he might face.

He decided to return to his previous life and to search for a new job. After a long search, Mr. Crab found work as a cook in a fancy restaurant.

RESUME
MANAGER

Year by year, he began to rise in his job until he achieved one of his aims. He became a famous chef, and he was able to buy his own restaurant too!

RESTAURANT

RESTAURANT
WELCOME